12-10-83

Santa
and
Alex

Santa and Alex

Delia Ephron
Illustrated by Elise Primavera

Little, Brown and Company
Boston   Toronto

Books by Delia Ephron

How to Eat Like a Child: & Other Lessons in Not Being a Grown-up
Teenage Romance: Or How to Die of Embarrassment
Santa and Alex

TEXT COPYRIGHT © 1983 BY DELIA EPHRON
ILLUSTRATIONS COPYRIGHT © 1983 BY ELISE PRIMAVERA

FIRST EDITION

Library of Congress Cataloging in Publication Data

Ephron, Delia.
  Santa and Alex.

  Summary: Alex has a very unusual adventure when he
decides to wait up for Santa Claus on Christmas Eve.
  [1. Santa Claus — Fiction. 2. Christmas — Fiction]
I. Primavera, Elise, ill. II. Title.
PZ7.E7246San 1983   [E]   83-14848
ISBN 0-316-24300-0
ISBN 0-316-24301-9 (pbk.)

AHS

*Published simultaneously in Canada
by Little, Brown & Company (Canada) Limited*

PRINTED IN THE UNITED STATES OF AMERICA

To Adam, Julie, and their dad

It was Christmas Eve. Alex had been in bed for hours, tucked in with his favorite bear. But he was too excited to sleep. He turned over on his tummy. He flipped back on his back. He wiggled and wiggled and wiggled until he got his blankets all messed up. "I can't fall asleep. I'll never fall asleep! Just think," he said to his bear, "Santa's out there flying through the sky with my presents."

Alex sat up; then he scrambled onto his knees so he could peek out the window. He searched the night sky as far as he could see. "Where are you, Santa? I wish you would come down the chimney now!"

Alex looked at his bear. "You know what?" he said. "We're going to get up and wait for Santa."

He picked up his bear and tiptoed to the door of his room. Slowly and carefully, so he would not make a sound, he opened it. The hallway was silent and dark. Even though Alex was sometimes afraid of the dark, he tiptoed bravely down the hall, past his sleeping cat, and past his parents' bedroom. "We're the only ones awake in this whole house," whispered Alex, as they sneaked into the living room.

"Now," he said, "where should we hide?"

Alex was stumped. They could hide behind the Christmas tree, but what if Santa spotted them while putting out the presents? He might go right back up the chimney and take Alex's presents with him.

"I know!" said Alex. He pulled the cushions off the couch, and, in the corner, across from the fireplace and in the shadow of a potted plant, he built a fort. "We're safe here," he said, taking his bear and crouching behind the cushions.

They waited. It was absolutely quiet. The light of the moon, shining through the window, played tricks with the Christmas tree, turning it from green to a silvery gray. Alex hugged his bear and hummed a little so he wouldn't get scared. He must have hummed himself right to sleep because he awoke with a start. The windows were rattling as if someone were trying to get in. Then they blew open and banged against the wall as a wind tore through the room. A vase of flowers crashed over; a lamp spun like a top. Alex himself was whipped into the air and almost right out of the house but he held on tight to the wall of his fort. Then, as suddenly as it had started, the wind ceased, and the room grew very cold and very still.

Clink-clink, clink-clink. What was that? Clink-clink, clink-clink. Alex looked up at the ceiling. It was coming from the roof, he was sure. Clink-clink, clink-clink, clink-clink. Was it the reindeer? Alex's heart thumped with excitement. He shot a look over the cushions. At any moment Santa would be here.

And they waited. "Come on, Santa," he thought. "Hurry up."

But Santa didn't come.

"What's taking you so long? I want to see you!"

No Santa.

Alex began to think he hadn't really heard the reindeer at all, he'd just imagined it. Then he got worried. Maybe Santa got stuck in the chimney.

"I'd better investigate," said Alex. He poked his head in the fireplace. "Santa," he called, "are you stuck up there?" No answer. He crawled in farther.

"Santa?" It was awfully dark and sooty. Alex could hardly see. He felt around with his hands. Some of the chimney bricks were smooth and even, but some poked out. "I could climb them like a ladder. I could climb the chimney!" And he did! Up to one brick. Then another. And another.

Whoa! Alex suddenly stopped. "What if Santa comes down while I'm going up and lands on my head? Uh-oh," thought Alex, "I'd better get out of here."

He started down. Oops — one foot slipped, then the other. "Help! Help!" Head over heels he tumbled. Upside down, right side up. "Help!!!!" Faster and faster he spun — so fast he didn't realize he wasn't falling down the chimney at all. He was falling up it. Whoosh! — Alex shot up the chimney and out the top. Way up into the sky. He did three somersaults, a back flip, and landed in a heap on —

"Excuse me, I'm not a horse, you know."

"What?" Alex was stunned. He looked to see what he was sitting on.

"I'm not a horse," it said again, and bucked, tumbling Alex off.

"Oh!" gasped Alex. Before him was a reindeer, stranger than any he had ever seen. Its antlers glowed like Christmas-tree lights. They blinked off and on and changed colors just like the lights on Alex's tree. Alex knew what his grandmother would say if she saw antlers like that. "Fancy, schmantzy," she'd say. "Fancy, schmantzy!"

Alex was so busy watching the antlers turn orange, the very same color as the Popsicle he'd eaten for lunch, that for a second, he didn't notice the other reindeer. He knew *them* all right because they were famous. "Hi, Dasher," said Alex. "Hi, Dancer. Hi, Prancer and Vixen and Comet and Cupid and Donner and Blitzen." Each reindeer bobbed his head and jingled the bells on his harness.

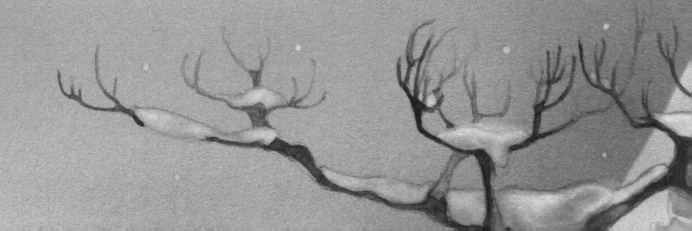

"And what about me?" said the reindeer whose antlers were now the color of a lime lollipop.

"You?" said Alex, shyly.

"What?" said the reindeer. "I didn't hear that. Did you hear that, Dasher?"

"No," said Dasher, turning to Dancer. "Did you?"

"No," said Dancer, turning to Prancer. "Did you?"

"No," said Prancer, turning to Vixen, Comet, Cupid, Donner, and Blitzen. "Did you?"

"No!" they shouted. And all the reindeer stared at Alex.

"I said," said Alex, speaking up as bravely as he could and using his best manners, "I don't think I know you."

"That's impossible," said the reindeer.

Impossible? Alex didn't know what to say. He knew he'd never heard of a reindeer with green — oops, now they were purple — antlers. Still, he didn't want to hurt the reindeer's feelings. "I must have forgotten," said Alex.

"Humpf," said the reindeer. "I can't imagine how." He drew himself up as tall as he could. His antlers shone as black as licorice. "My name is Jeremy."

"Jeremy?" said Alex. "But that's not a reindeer name."

"Not a reindeer name!"

"Excuse me," said Alex, even more confused. "It's just that I have a friend at school named Jeremy."

"I suppose you think my name should be Twinkle. Or Swifty. Do you have any friends at school named Twinkle or Swifty?" Jeremy didn't wait for an answer. "I suppose that the only other reindeer you know is that one with the red nose. I won't mention his name but I call him Fat Nose. The boss isn't using him this year, he's using me!"

The boss! Alex had almost forgotten. He ran over to the sleigh. It was empty, except in the back, where he saw an enormous sack. "Where's Santa?" asked Alex.

"Your guess is as good as mine," said Jeremy, as his antlers lit up a yummy raspberry. "We land on a roof, and the next thing I know, I can't find him anywhere."

"He's going to deliver my presents, isn't he?"

"What else would we be doing here?" said Jeremy. The other reindeer giggled.

At that moment Jeremy's antlers flashed two colors at once — velvety brown at the bottom and frosty white at the tips. They made Alex think of his favorite dessert.

"It's not polite to stare," said Jeremy.

"I didn't mean to," said Alex, "but right now your antlers look like chocolate pudding and whipped cream."

"My antlers what????" said Jeremy.

Alex watched the antlers blink off, then twinkle pink. "Now they're just like bubble gum," said Alex.

"Bubble gum! My antlers! I've never been so insulted!" And Jeremy stuck his nose in the air and refused even to look at Alex.

"Oh, Jeremy," said Alex. "I like your antlers. I love them! I think they're —" and Alex tried to think of the nicest words he could. "I think they're fancy, schmantzy."

"Fancy, schmantzy?" said Jeremy. He turned to Dasher. "What do you think?"

"Fancy, schmantzy," said Dasher, turning to Dancer. "What do you think?"

"Fancy, schmantzy," said Dancer, turning to Prancer. "What do you think?"

"Fancy, schmantzy," said Prancer, turning to Vixen, Comet, Cupid, Donner, and Blitzen. "What do you think?"

"Fancy, schmantzy!" they shouted.

"I guess they are," said Jeremy, tossing his head proudly. "I bet you wish you had antlers like mine."

Alex was about to agree, even though he thought he'd look pretty funny with antlers on his head, when something bopped him. "What was that?"

"Up to his tricks," said Jeremy. "Better duck."

"Who?" asked Alex, as another snowball whizzed over his shoulder.

Before Jeremy could answer, Alex heard, from behind the chimney, "Ho, ho, ho!"

"Santa Claus?" cried Alex.

"Ho, ho, ho!" This time the voice was behind Alex, whispering right in his ear. Alex jumped and turned around.

And there was Santa — more roly-poly than Alex had ever imagined. He wore his red suit with white fur trim. He had a long white beard, a rosy nose, and a jolly face. Santa leaned over and said very slowly, "Helllll-o." His breath in the cold air made a ring of vapor, which Santa twirled on his finger. "Want a doughnut?" he asked.

Before Alex could answer, the ring had evaporated and Santa was chuckling, holding his belly as it shook. Alex could see that Santa liked to have a good time.

"Well," said Santa, "you must be Alex."

"Yes," said Alex.

22

"And what are you doing on the roof in the middle of the night without your jacket?"

Uh-oh. Alex didn't want Santa to get mad at him. "I fell up the chimney," he said.

"You fell up the chimney, eh? You hear that, Jeremy?"

"Humpf," said Jeremy, turning to Dasher. "Did you hear that?"

"Humpf," said Dasher, turning to Dancer. "Did you hear that?"

"Humpf," said Dancer, turning to Prancer —

"That's enough boys," said Santa, chuckling. He picked up Alex and sat down on the chimney with Alex on his knee. "Scratch me here," said Santa, pointing to his cheek just above his beard. Alex tickled Santa's cheek. Lickety-split, Santa growled and snapped at Alex's finger, scaring Alex and making him jump, but making him giggle, too.

"Could you do that again?" said Alex.

But this time Santa said, "Raise your hand and spell 'up' backwards."

Alex thought. He knew "up" was spelled U-P. So he raised his hand and said, "P.U."

"Oh," said Alex, very embarrassed, realizing what Santa had tricked him into saying. Santa started laughing again. His belly shook. Even his knee shook, which made Alex bounce up and down. Alex couldn't help it, he started laughing, too.

"Hey, Santa," said Alex, pointing to the sky. "Look over there."

Santa looked.

"Made you look, made you look, made you buy a penny book," chanted Alex. "I got you that time, didn't I, Santa?"

Santa started chuckling. His face got red. "Ho, ho, ho, ho, ho, ho, ho." He couldn't stop. Alex couldn't help staring at Santa's belly, which really did shake like jelly. "You got me all right," said Santa, wiping some tears of laughter from his eyes.

"Boss," said Jeremy in a scolding voice, "are we delivering presents or aren't we? Is this Christmas Eve or isn't it?"

"Hold on to your horns, Jeremy," said Santa, winking at Alex. "We're just having some fun."

Jeremy snorted and stamped his hoof. His antlers glowed like two bright yellow bananas.

"Can I go with you, Santa? Can I deliver presents, too?" asked Alex.

"No," said Santa.

"Please," said Alex. "Please. I won't be in the way, I really won't. I'll just be a help."

"No." Santa shook his head.

Alex's lips began to quiver. He didn't mean to cry, but he wanted to go so much.

"No means yes and yes means no!" boomed Santa, whisking Alex into the air and popping him into the sleigh.

"No means yes — I can go!" cried Alex, amazed.

Santa hopped into the sleigh beside him. "But you must make me a promise, Alex." For the first time, Santa spoke very seriously.

"I will," said Alex.

"You must promise that you will never tell anyone. It must be our secret forever and ever."

"I promise, Santa. I'll never tell anyone, ever, ever, ever," said Alex.

"Shake," said Santa, sticking out his hand to seal the bargain.

Alex put out his hand. Santa shook it, poked Alex in the ribs, and then tweaked Alex's ear, chanting, "Shake-speare, pat on the ear." Then Santa started chuckling all over again. Alex started giggling again, too.

"Do it again," he said.

"No time," said Santa. He tucked a blanket around Alex. Then he shook the reins and whistled. In a jingle of bells, the sleigh rose into the sky.

Alex's heart skipped as the sleigh sailed higher and higher. "Hi, moon. Hi, stars." Alex waved; then he sneaked up close to Santa.

As they flew through the night, Santa sang a song that sounded like "Turkey in the Straw" but went like this:

> Oh, I had a little chicken and she wouldn't lay an egg,
> So I poured hot water up and down her leg,
> And the little chicken cried,
> And the little chicken begged,
> And the gosh darn chicken laid a hard-boiled egg.

Each time Santa finished the song, Alex giggled and said, "Sing it again, Santa." And Santa did.

By the time the sleigh landed on the first house, Alex was very excited. "Stop jumping up and down this minute, Alex," said Santa, "you might fall out." Then, to Alex's surprise, Santa picked him up and popped him inside the sack of presents. Santa slung the sack over his shoulder, and Alex rode down the chimney with the presents.

No sooner had Alex crawled out of the sack than Santa dove into it, burying himself right up to his belly. Presents began to shoot out into Alex's arms. One even landed on his head and sat there like a hat. Quickly, Alex laid the presents under the tree. "I'm really helping, aren't I, Santa?" said Alex, looking up just in time to see Santa scoot over to the mantel and fill up the stockings.

"You sure are," said Santa. He gave Alex two of the cookies the children had left for him.

"I bet you're going to leave me a lot of presents when we go back to my house!" said Alex. "Aren't you?"

"Let me see your hand," said Santa.

He took Alex's hand and studied his palm very seriously. "Oh-ho," he said, "I see a house." He looked even closer. "Inside that house I see a mean witch who doesn't like anybody or anything. She is so mean she doesn't want children playing near her house. So do you know what this wicked witch does?"

"What?" said Alex.

"She puts up a sign right here," said Santa, pointing to the center of Alex's hand. "And that sign says, 'If you want presents for Christmas, keep off the grass.'" Santa paused. "Now where did she put that sign? I forget."

"Here," said Alex, touching the spot on his hand that Santa had pointed to.

"Keep off the grass! Keep off the grass! Keep off the grass!" shouted Santa, pretending to be the witch and tickling Alex. Alex collapsed, giggling and squirming.

"Do it again!" said Alex.

But Santa was slinging the sack of presents over his shoulder. "Hold on to my coat," he said.

Alex grabbed Santa's jacket with both hands. "Don't let go," said Santa, placing a finger next to his nose. Santa nodded. Up the chimney he rose, pulling Alex up with him.

On the roof Jeremy waited, his antlers red as a red-hot cinnamon candy. "Playing pinochle, boss?" he said, very irritated.

"Hold on to your horns, Jeremy, we're off," said Santa, as he and Alex hopped back into the sleigh.

"Hold on to your horns," said Dasher, giggling.

"Hold on to your horns," said Dancer, giggling.

"Hold on to your horns," said Prancer —

"That's enough, boys," said Santa. He shook the reins and whistled. Off they went again.

Far and wide they traveled. Up and down chimney after chimney, they delivered presents and ate cookies until finally Alex couldn't help it — he yawned.

Santa saw and winked. Then he whistled three sharp trills.

"Why did you do that?" asked Alex.

Santa put his finger to his lips, signaling that Alex should be quiet and see. The sleigh began to circle. With each loop it dropped lower, coming closer and closer to a cloud, then landing on it very gently.

"It's time to go home," said Santa.

"But I don't want to," said Alex.

"Remember," said Santa, "you must never tell anyone that you came with me."

Alex nodded solemnly.

"Shake," said Santa, sticking out his hand. Alex shook it. Santa poked him in the ribs, tweaked his ear, and said, "Shake-speare, pat on the ear." Alex started giggling. "I'm telling on you, Santa," he said.

"Why?" said Santa, quite surprised.

" 'Cause you put ants in my pants and you made me do the doggy dance!"

"What?" said Santa, throwing up his hands and pretending to be shocked.

" 'Cause you put rocks in my socks and you gave me chicken pox!" cried Alex, so excited he was jumping up and down.

"What?!" said Santa, even louder, as though he couldn't believe his ears.

" 'Cause you put beans in my jeans and sent me to New Orleans!" shrieked Alex, feeling so silly and happy that he jumped into Santa's arms.

"Ho, ho, ho, ho, ho," chuckled Santa. He hugged Alex tight.

Over Santa's shoulder, Alex saw a star floating toward them. The star, brighter than any other star in the sky, glittered as though it had been showered with gold. Closer and closer it came.

"The star will take you home," whispered Santa.

But Alex clung to Santa, hugging him as hard as he could. "Don't be scared," said Santa softly, kissing Alex good-bye.

"Good-bye, Santa," said Alex. "Good-bye, Jeremy. Good-bye, Dasher and Dancer and Prancer and Vixen and Comet and Cupid and Donner and Blitzen." The reindeer jingled their bells. Jeremy's antlers lit up like peppermint sticks.

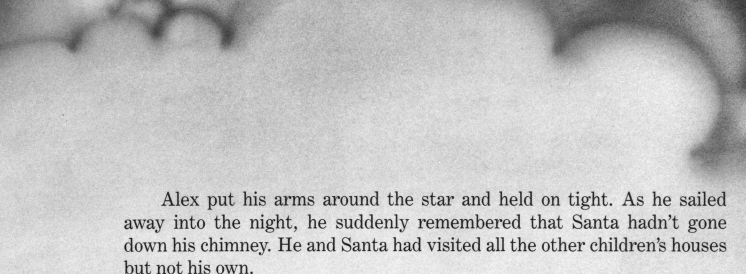

Alex put his arms around the star and held on tight. As he sailed
away into the night, he suddenly remembered that Santa hadn't gone
down his chimney. He and Santa had visited all the other children's houses
but not his own.

"Santa," yelled Alex, "you forgot my house! You forgot me!" But
Santa was far away and couldn't hear him.

"You forgot me!" cried Alex as loud as he could.

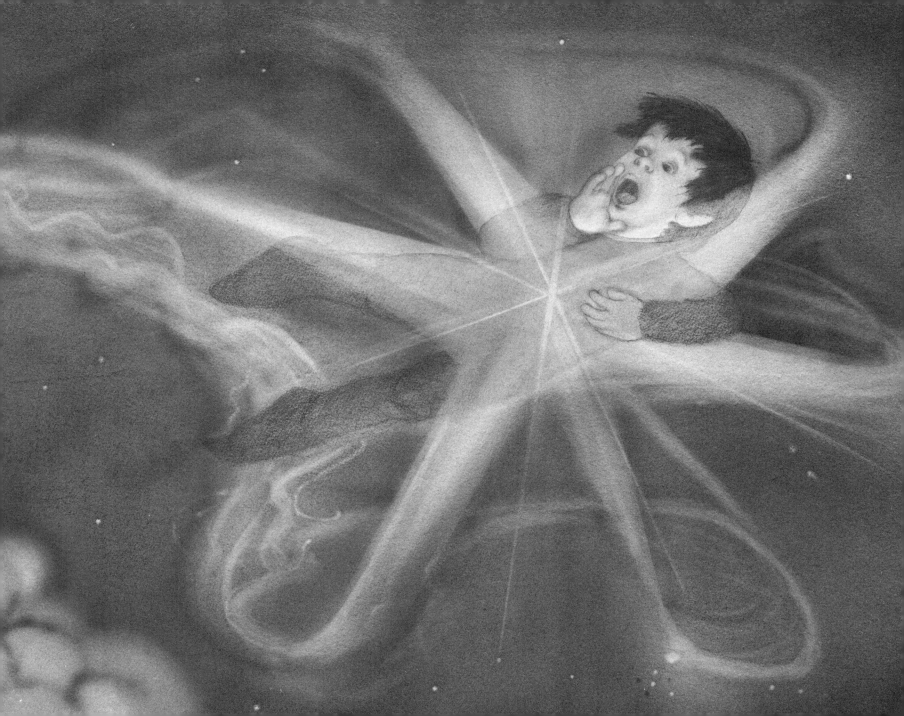

The next thing Alex knew it was morning, and he was in bed. Uh-oh — his presents! Alex threw off the covers and raced into the living room. And there they all were, under the tree — every gift that Alex had wished for. "Hurrah!" cried Alex. "Santa did remember!"

But where was his bear? Alex looked around. "Bear?" he called. Then he found him, tucked behind the potted plant, sound asleep.

Alex grabbed his bear and hugged him, and that was when he saw it. Pinned to his bear was a star. Santa's star. It glittered as though it had been showered with gold.

Alex never told anyone what happened to him that Christmas Eve. He kept the secret for the rest of his life.